Rainmaker

This book
was donated by

Robert L. Nugent, Ph.D.
1920-2012

Professor Emeritus
of Modern Languages

Director of the
James F. Lincoln Library

Rainmaker

Jan Östergren

Translated
by
John Matthias
and
Göran Printz-Påhlson

Ohio University Press
Athens, Ohio
London

Translation © Copyright 1983 by John Matthias and Göran Printz-Påhlson

These poems were originally published in *Boeing 707 och andra dikter, Regnmakare, Indiansommar,* and *Travers mellan ordprakt och förfall,* all by Bo Cavefors Bokförlag

Printed in the United States of America.
All rights reserved.

Library of Congress Cataloging in Publication Data

Östergren, Jan, 1940–
   Rainmaker.

   I. Title.
PT9876.25.E67A26   1983   839.7'174   82-24554
ISBN 0-8214-0745-7
ISBN 0-8214-0746-5 (pbk.)

Contents

Note and Acknowledgments..........................vii

Part One.. 1

    Contemporary............................ 3
    Indian Summer I........................13

Part Two..19

    Motto................................. 21
    The Epochs............................22
    Morning, light........................25
    Fable................................. 26
    The Attempt...........................27
    Dry Point.............................28
    Rainstorm............................. 29
    Burning Stubble.......................30
    Nature Morte..........................31
    View, tempera.........................32
    Inspection............................ 33
    from *From a Table in Europe*..............34

Part Three..37

    Words................................. 39
    Love.................................. 42
    Death................................. 47
    Indian Summer II......................49

Note and Acknowledgments

The poems by Jan Östergren translated in this volume are drawn from *Boeing 707 och andra dikter*, *Regnmakare*, *Indiansommar*, and *Travers mellan ordprakt och förfall*, all published in Sweden by Bo Cavefors Bokförlag. Grateful acknowledgment is made to the author and publisher for permission to publish these translations. For readers acquainted with the Swedish texts, we should make it clear that several of these poems are translated from versions which differ in some details from their appearance in Mr. Östergren's books. The poems in question are "Burning Stubble," "Nature Morte," "Death," section II (1) of "Contemporary," and sections I(3) and I(5) of "Indian Summer." Some of these translations have previously appeared in *Chicago Review, Poetry and Audience, Modern Poetry in Translation, The Greenfield Review,* and *Contemporary Swedish Poetry*.

Part One

Contemporary

(1.)

Somewhere
moving on towards
earth *technology* em-
ulates its
origin: in man

      The aircraft
overtakes, overcomes
the palpi-
tations of its heart

slides against us
on a single wheel, a single edge
(like a skater's)
    perfect
    landing!

    stopping
just before the heart
bangs its way on out
of its sheet-
metal skin

(2.)

Taking off once more:
man the fellow-
traveller drags at first
hangs in strata of the air
      soon is fully-
fledged as bird: like the merganser
in wild flight with
the cordite stain around
its quillfeathers

Up from here
in one big hurry!
Higher up
there somewhere, on the move
away from earth mankind
emulates *technology*   pushes off
with the garbled speech
of radar: frictions

pulse in center:
drilling
in the sheath
of frontal veins

(3.)

round round
a metalplated re-
volving door
between the cockles of
his heart, round round

the New Man
towards the old goal
chugging
along

the standard dream
just for a second
left behind   hovering
in transit: (short of breath)
the Volvo
and Alsatians in the trunk

      there's no place
for tolerance here: not even
repressive: only good
behavior's boarding
card: a haymaker
straight to the solar plexus

all the other senses
behind a protective
nose-cone

(4.)

O Icarus!

Takes off and topples
right in the sea.
In a quarter of an hour: The scramble
from here   Water
hollows stone   hollows the trunk
(man) hol-
lows his own self!

Washing pad. Christening font.
The coming-hither
is the mirage: Blinded!

Dither,
tumbling helter-skelter
like tracers
above the ecstasy
the materialist

apocalypsis

(5.)

Sorry Customs
nothing to
declare
bar the poems
in my breast: in-
finitely carefully
folded para-
chute jumps
        fractions

of silence
Yrs & Mine

Let's wake up
let's never fall asleep
away from each other

or:
let's fall asleep
don't wake up
away from me!

II
(1.)

Suburban bus
chugging along
like a steamer
laboriously turns
the corner, its belly
full of rain
& tired eyes

sum:
78 X Jonah

Death at a distance
dressed in a black topcoat
disperses among the colors
& the houses, the secular
and stingy

Patent-leather shoes!
(in the display window)
did you see it glisten
Citizen? the glittering
heel of Charon

(2.)

With a poet's
self-assumed right
I'm interfering with
your mind   you

who doesn't understand
who doesn't want to—and always
has a common life
to run   I

want to take care
of your language
prevent an extra uterine
pregnancy   I

shall prescribe an incubator
for the dialogue   we
cannot clarify the world
with signal flags

(3.)

Not to be burning
in the furnace
of the sun
at twelve o' clock

Not to be snared
in darkness
by a howling
crazy moon

somewhere
inbetween there is
an area of probability
to be regained: to
recapture
life, life-
lines

regain language,
pour it out like silver
into melting pots, coining
the new values

I'm not foisting
off on you
my inner life
(idol-atry)

at the very best I want
to start your own!

(4.)

Mankind inter-
connected
polyphonic: in
many voices We

we are all
reciprocally
marked: a choir
of collective
solos

layer on top
layer which forms
patterns—imprints
of each other's
lonelinesses

to map existence
visibly
with tricks of illusion

to seek each other
with our fingertips, to offer
one another
long lost pieces of the puzzle

(5.)

We must say *no*
deep down
at the bottom: feel
the scraping
under the dinghy

let
ourselves be *dematerialized*
even if it is against
our will: closer
to each other now
even now

& maintain this
with words, yes why not
with words?

We're all
inside us rowing
for our lives
in a boat race

tantalizingly near
each other—side by side
in the poem:
Simultaneousdinghy

We are all!

Indian Summer I
(1.)

Ships
belching in the night
like deer in fog
have butted
at the quay

The morning
rolls in sun & light
on a hay wain
through the east gate: gaping
in the black barn
of night

      :out rush
the dreams

nightmare bursts
in the pale light

(2.)

The kelp-
gatherer urges on
his mare: leaves
the wagon tracks to heal
slowly in marsh-
lands

Far out
at the horizon
the sun has put
its warming earthen jug
in the sea

(3.)

To be a piece
in fertility's profit-
able crisscrossing
shuffle of scuffs

Humming
bicycle tires, pockets
full of
despair, these
compass needles every-
where in the body

No—never
again any more:

The hare among
the wolfhounds

    :the Child
breaks out of the circle
and veers towards
age with head-
lights
in his rear-view mirror

(4.)

I
am waiting for
the moment when the hare
furiously turns
around   and
the hounds flee
to the woods
with short bob-
tailed pulses

I
want to expose
the gaps in
the training
     want to show
the panic in the poodle-
wise, taught

     want to chase
the commonplaces
off to the woods, out
of reach

(5.)

    escapes
like the vortex
of sunlight
through the clearing

like
the flame under
a magnifying lens

In the time of re-
fractions
the sun glass is
my ocular:
my sixth
pyrotechnical
sense

      but when
the underbrush
crackles
with fire—
then like the deer
I believe
in new escapes

in the soft wild-
ness between
the trunks of trees

Part Two

Motto

—once again
bring into light
the battle painting
hanging concealed
in every man

Austere days
simple mottos are better
than none at all

The Epochs
(1.)

The discarded combine-
harvester, a corroding
Bristol fighter
from World War I

abandoned implements,
the narrow hulls of ploughs
burrowing in the clay
—shipwrecks!
everywhere

Some may say: O bury
all this rusting junk at once!
And others:—not
too deep though. Think of
History

to be exhumed again
in a few thousand years
A new Iron Age,
if we're still around

Today we'll be his-
torical: Use the lanuage
which the earth
has just forgotten

Cattle
blowing still
their horns of bronze

(2.)

In America they had
artificial rains, already
in the 1940s

they flew up
and fertilized the clouds
with frozen CO_2

Then tailor-made rains
started falling
on John Ford's movie sets

but never a drop
—upon
the Grapes of Wrath

(3.)

Well ok! on the Homestead

—whatever happened
to the hydraulic Sunnybrook Farms
which you celebrated in those poems
of the 1920s

the oily pistons
which were to unburden
man, sure enough
—where did they go?

You
ravenous
visionaries

observe depression
brooding over the downs,
and—the Reactor!

Morning, light

In October
aging is
tender, faint

carefully, the wind
sorts out old leaves
under the copper beach

& rain froth shines
in the copper ear
of the gutter—white

down, of the nuances
& the flute
intern me now!

Fable

After the meal
we allow ourselves
a smoke

The magpies
squabble in the grass,
nick the cutlery

obdurate birds,
crazy for loot
like people

—the same
lacquered laughter
of hammered tin!

The Attempt

To break loose
—stone slab
from stone

—pare down,
hewing & hammering
address, or

why not
caress out of it
a piece of life

quarry life!
in our warm
hands

—bend
the unbending
thou & I

into *we*
in the bowl
of our palms

I speak you
a picture with words
visible

address is
at least attempt,
half a dialogue

Dry Point

This time of year
autumn gnaws
at the porch

all the junipers
seem to be drafted into
the home guard

In the meadow
the butcher
already has switched on
a deep-freeze mist
around the cattle

Rainstorm

The wind sniffing
around the house,
moulding leaves

slamming doors,
hooking all the shutters

The Viggen jet turns round,
dives like a crazy fiddle bow
into the back of a cloud

—after a while
the rain begins to pound:
millions of soft knuckles
on the corrugated roof

inside
is dry, but hotter
than Kenya

Burning Stubble

Flames,
searing wolves' tongues
ran across the fields
a little away
from the houses

the firemen's
growling red tomcat
lept
when the last drop
of water sizzled
in its fur—

the old harvest
the old world
burned

singed away a day
from my thirty years

Nature Morte

What does it help? lank
cucumbers' green prattle
about the processes—
air, darkness, light

—autumn has
its own revolt,
its own mild
anarchy

like the cran-
berries have their cellar's
life in the crock
all winter long

View, tempera

A sea bird: absolutely still
in the breeze
Waiting for a bearing & ex-
pecting a veering of the wind
to have its will

Lands squawking
Presses out some pea-green lumps
Curtsies—and disappears
in rapid brush strokes across
a sea-green canvas

Inspection

The blackbird's
stepping along, a dark
presence sent here
with a Geiger counter
in its beak

that's what makes
the crawler
keep its profile low,
following the mine-
shaft: Patience

until he lifts off
like a natural law

from From a Table in Europe

*

A column of army trucks
passes by.
Europe drives its herds
toward new pastures,
new hearths—
against whom
and why?

Old peasant women
draw together: black eyes
dart around
like frightened swallows,
meet the strategic stare
of the officer in charge—
and kill him!
silently—in their hearts
a thousand times.

Why this
endless caravan
loaded with salt
for open wounds?

This destructive potential
tuned in forges
and rifle ranges—
where life is calibrated
with nerve gas

Where the nights are white
from shrapnel and tracers
and the day black
like a death ramp.

*

The snowflake struck
by a flash of summer lightning—
in this way couple
death & life

I am thinking of
your heart's silver bell,
its precise little beats,
its supremacy!

Paul Celan—
from all the electrodes
of anguish
and the lead cosh of the commandant
finally free
in the brown water of the Seine

For you I draw
the fastest arrow shaft
from my quiver

Hear—
the bow is singing
its purest
song

Look—
the arrow turns into a bird
a bobbing thrush
in the Bois de Boulogne

We shall never meet.

You should have chosen
a sea of royal
blue—
the sailor wrapped
in his spinnaker

*

In the smoky morning mist
under sorrowful oaks
Van Ruyjsdal's cattle stood
with bursting udders
lowing
like fog horns
across the enormous
sea of meadows

The horse
majestically alone
dipped his muzzle
into a warm nose bag

Brittle sun
and mist
lay entangled
in the soft duel
of dawn

Part Three

Words

(1.)

When I write words
I don't mean silent
snowflakes on slate-
warm roofs,

I mean
indoors: Firewood. Everybody's
his own tiled stove   we
smoke for a while
before we can warm up
the others

    before we
can follow the smoke
through your soft
filter, cloud of words

(2.)

To live is
to take risks
somewhere an-
chored at the bottom
of language

the retreat back-
wards towards all
circumstances'
rock bottom
beginning

pry open
the blue mussel
when she rock-
silent keeps
shut

break
your gob
halfway out of joint
in the oyster-
bank

(3.)

Deeply inside
I believe
in the words

the nuances
the prac-
ticalities

Yes:
we notice
broom by its smell
—in spite of all
this prattle
about yellowness!

listen to our
songs: smell of flowers
groping out of
the larynx

lips
in darkness: read them

Love

(1.)

When
I write love
I don't mean
Goethe's 150 year old
sleight of hand: the quill
as bootjack

and not the Spanish
cloak under which
passion rises with the
rank of ensign

I mean:
the little fugue
squeezed through the
teeth of the organ—soon to be free!

sonata
for winds
and clouds

(2.)

Keeeez me hot meeezter
she said blue with cold, lips
like candied violets

Zing de lazzt danzz
she said later on
and started to
take off her clothes

Baby doll
eager on the
outside but

deep inside chaste
as a display window   wanted
only her innocence back

become new
like a season: every
winter new ice
on the canal

(3.)

Our desire
a dipping butterfly
which we catch, own
for a moment

        our

brain
a free habitation
for the softest
whims

        we

can afford
that
luxury

        our

heart
in one
single pulse-beat
we strike through
fall asleep under

open skies
tonight

(4.)

Childwoman
with desires
swimming in your
inner oceans

let us probe
the deep
with each other

You have depth
I have plummet
and weights

we who have shared
the slumber of the child
heavy and warm
in the diving bell

let us return
to the surface: con-
quer the world
together

you have winds
I have sails

(5.)

Let us disembark
across the drawbridge bent
like a backbone under
the past

let us forget
the past

let us build
each other new
at the shoreline

:a
gothic arch
which weightless
catches rhythms
of the flute

Death

(1.)

Once you wanted
to talk about life
& started with death

:Blue Gillette,
the powerless words
in the bathroom cupboard

Paul Celan!

you taught me
to weigh life
on scales of gold: it had
to be right!

even if we lie
a gram here & there
we have to preserve
It All

:death,
a torpedo
in the net of the trawler

(2.)

*Your laughter is a dagger
honed for Garcia Lorca*

In a stable
with whitewashed stalls
I heard a donkey bray

as mangily
    as brutishly
as laughter
in a crematory

will never forget
my delight
when I thought: this
ought to be brayed out
every sunday for
centuries
to come

would have saved us
many an evangelical
flight

Indian Summer II
(1.)

I do not split
atoms, do not divide
my life
in two   in heart
or brain
either
or

if you say
either-or
my answer is
both-ways!

if you say
black-or-white,
then I will split the atom
in words

in life: a gospel
for us to play
together, try to stop it
if you dare

I'm putting
a jack-screw
behind my words

(2.)

The words
slip away
slide
chafing like boot-straps
when we are roaming about
to the mill
filled up by defectives
my Remington
and I

but toss them
under stone, Miller
grind them: the words
into pure flour

if they'll ever do

(3.)

Imagination: our only
absolute freedom

the mainspring,
the chimney-smoke
straight as an arrow
defying reality's day-
light, vertical

though bent
and broken at last
against the horizon: of
the real

& falling beneath
our eyes, standing there
like smudges in the crust
on the snow

we do it and
we do it once again
    tryout

we will never
come closer
to a breathing house

(4.)

Your heart
is a team of Oxen,
your arteries & veins
a wagon track
against the wind

whimpering spokes
Life like waving
grass

a green hub
against
earth's gravity

and so?

You have swallows
in your wagon,
who
is afraid of
the earth?